fimbles™

Tambourine

BBC

Florrie and Baby Pom were playing a game of copying in the Purple Meadow.

"Florrie says clap your hands!" said Florrie.

Baby Pom clapped her hands and then she stopped.

"Florrie says keep clapping!" said Florrie.

"Hello you two," said Bessie

from the branch above. "Can I join in?"

"Oh yes, please," said Florrie.

"Baby Pom isn't very good

at this game."

Bessie joined in the game and did exactly as Florrie told her.
First she nodded her head, then she flapped her wings.
"Flappety flap-flap-flap," said Bessie, and flew off.

"Florrie says goodbye," chuckled Florrie.
Baby Pom decided to run off, too.
When Florrie realized she
was alone, she called,
"Florrie says come back!"

Florrie decided to look for Baby Pom. On her way to the Purple Meadow, she got the Fimbling Feeling.

"I can feel a twinkling,
I can hear a sound,
It's telling me there's something
Waiting to be found!
Where is it? Where is it?
What could it be?
I think it might be over there,
Let's go and see!"

"I like this," said Florrie, as she shook the circular jingly thing she had found.

It made a lovely rattling sound...

...and when she put her arm through it, it made a big bracelet!
"Fimbo! Pom! Come and see what I've found!" she called.
"A tambourine!" Florrie ran off to find them.

Over at the Bubble Fall, Fimbo was shaking his
Shimmy Shaker and Rockit was dancing.
Baby Pom stood watching them.

"Shimmy, shimmy, shimmy, shimmy.
Shake-shake-shake!" chanted Fimbo.

"Limy, limy,
limy, limy.
Lake-lake-lake!"
chanted Rockit.

"Ooh! Rattle-tattle, jingle-jangle, shake-shake-shake!" laughed Rockit.

"There you are!" said Florrie. "I've found a tambourine."
"You can shake it or bang it, you can even put it on your arm,
or on your nose...

...you can even put it on your head to make a crown.
Greetings – I'm Queen Florrie!"

"Queen Florrie says it's your turn to bow now, Fimbo,"
said Florrie, with a smile.

Fimbo bowed. "Greetings, Your Majesty," he said.

Baby Pom wanted to copy Fimbo, so she bowed as well.

"Let's pretend I'm a real queen," cried Florrie.

"Yes, Your Majesty, of course, Your Majesty," said Rockit.

Fimbo found some material for Florrie to wear as a robe.

Queen Florrie sat down on her throne and asked the others to sing her a song.

Florrie tapped, and shook, and jangled her tambourine...

...while the others danced and sang.

Soon, Queen Florrie clapped her hands for everyone to stop. "I'm hungry," she said. "Bring me some crackers!"

Fimbo went to
find the crackers.

"And Pom, bring me Little One,"
said Queen Florrie. Baby Pom
didn't move.

"You know," said Queen
Florrie, "it's like the game
we were playing before."

But Baby Pom still didn't move.

Florrie sighed loudly, but Baby Pom still didn't move. When Fimbo came back nibbling the crackers, Queen Florrie grumbled at him.

"Those are the queen's crackers, not yours!"
"I was hungry," mumbled Fimbo.

Baby Pom wanted to try on the tambourine crown, but
Queen Florrie wouldn't let her.
So Baby Pom wandered off, and Fimbo went to find her.

Queen Florrie was all on her own.

Fimbo found Baby Pom and Rockit at the Busy Base.
   "I've had enough of that game," he said.
"Florrie is being such a bossy-boots."

"Princess Pom!" said Baby Pom.

"Good idea!" said Fimbo, and he looked around for materials to make a new crown.

Meanwhile, Florrie was still sitting on her throne wearing her tambourine crown.

She was all alone. Roly Mo popped his head up.

"Where are the others?" he asked.

"They've gone away," said Florrie. "We were playing a really good game where I was the Queen, but they just wouldn't do what I said."

Florrie was feeling sad. She didn't like being on her own. "Oh, Roly Mo. I think the others went away because I was being so bossy!" sighed Florrie. "I'd better find them and say sorry."

Back at the Busy Base, Baby Pom's crown
was looking wonderful.
   "We just need some jewels," said Fimbo.

"I like your crown!" said Rockit. "Are you going to be
King Fimbo?"

"No, it's for Baby Pom," explained Fimbo.

Florrie found the others at the Busy Base. Baby Pom was wearing her princess crown.

"I like your crown," said Florrie.

"Do you want my robe? I'm sorry I was so bossy. Can I play with you?" she asked.

"Yes!" said everyone.